The Legend of the
Putter Frog
of Frogmore, SC

by Randy Bazemore
illustrated by Warner McGee

Published by Clifton Carriage House Press, Minneapolis, MN,
a division of BRIO

BRIO
12 S. Sixth St. Suite 1250
Minneapolis, MN 55402

ISBN 978-0-9825713-7-8
LCCN: 2011929668

Art by Warner McGee

This story is dedicated to my wife, Wanda Horne Bazemore, my parents, Paul R. Bazemore, Sr. and Azilea Smith Bazemore (deceased), my  children, Bree Bazemore Welmaker, Bryan Paul Bazemore, and Tanner Rhea Bazemore, my step-daughter, Aaron May, and my grandchildren, Patrick Welmaker and Allyson Welmaker, Maela Bazemore, and Rachel May. Special thanks goes to Fred and Linda Bazemore for their support and friendship.

Once upon a time, in a faraway pond near Frogmore, South Carolina, there lived a papa frog and a mama frog who dreamed of someday having a family. After waiting and tending to many eggs, Mama and Papa Frog proudly watched as they turned into tadpoles. So many little tadpoles swimming round and round!

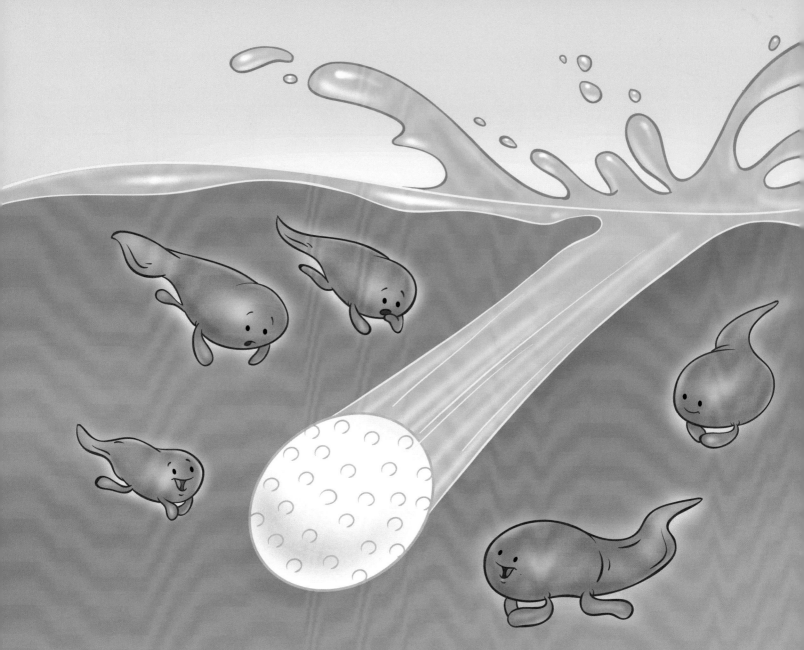

But one tadpole, the smallest, was different. Instead of playing with his brothers and sisters, he liked to watch people at the edge of the pond play a game. One day, as he watched, there was a loud SPLASH! Something white and round landed in the pond! The tiny tadpole swam around it, wondering what it could be, but before he could figure it out, a large hand reached into the pond and scooped the round thing up.

As each spring day passed and the tiny tadpole grew, he continued to watch people play the mysterious game. He was so intent on watching that he hardly noticed he was growing up. Now he was a little frog! He could use his new strong legs and arms to pull himself out of the water, just a little bit, to watch the game even more closely.

A few more weeks, the little frog was able to pull himself out of the pond completely and jump behind a bush at the edge of the fairway. He could hardly contain his excitement. This was a game he wanted to play, too!

But before the little frog could play, he needed to have the right equipment. He found a stick and shaped it to look like the clubs the players were using. Now all he needed was something to hit. It didn't take him long to spot a plump, round berry that was the same shape as the white round thing.

The little frog placed the berry on the grass facing the pond. He gripped the club he made and swung it, hitting the berry straight ahead. Whoosh! It soared through the air and landed smack in the middle of a lily pad. The berry made the perfect ball!

The little frog placed the berry on the grass facing the pond. He gripped the club he made and swung it, hitting the berry straight ahead. Whoosh! It soared through the air and landed smack in the middle of a lily pad. The berry made the perfect ball!

But before the little frog could play, he needed to have the right equipment. He found a stick and shaped it to look like the clubs the players were using. Now all he needed was something to hit. It didn't take him long to spot a plump, round berry that was the same shape as the white round thing.

Some of the little frog's brothers and sisters cheered him on from the pond's edge.

"Come on, Little Frog! Hit it all the way to the other side!" shouted one of his brothers.

And that is exactly what the little frog did—he hit the berry all the way across the pond.

The little frog swam to the pond's edge, got out of the water, and went to the berry. He set it several feet away from a hole in the grass and gently tapped it in. For the next one, he moved the berry a little further away and again, tapped it into the hole.

The little frog practiced every day and soon he was playing the game of golf, just like the people he had spent so much time watching!

Each afternoon when the sun started to fade, Mama Frog and Papa Frog would call the little frog back home to the pond for supper.

"Please let me play just a few more holes," begged the little frog. When Papa Frog responded with a loud "RIBBIT!" he knew he had to go home and probably would get a lecture from his parents.

Over supper, Mama Frog explained to the little frog that his brothers and sisters were studying hard to become doctor frogs, lawyer frogs, and even banker frogs. They did not want him to become a golfer frog!

"I promise I will study hard, but please let me continue to play golf," said the little frog.

"If you study hard and keep up with your chores, your mama and I will let you play golf," replied Papa Frog.

The little frog hopped up and hugged his parents.

After dinner when he was in bed, the little frog dreamed of playing eighteen holes of golf in a pond course made of lily pads. When he woke up the next morning, he knew he had to make this dream come true.

After doing his homework and chores, the little frog set out to build his new course. Going to each lily pad, he placed a flag at the end and put a little shell under the flags. He worked very hard, and by the time he finished the course, his brothers and sisters had lined up to watch what he would do next.

With his newly made clubs and bag, the little frog was ready to hit the berry ball to the first lily pad. Suddenly, a fly buzzed in front of him. He tried to swat it away.

The fly stopped in midair and yelled, "Hey dude, you can't hit me! I'm too fast! And you need some help playing golf! Just look at you—you're never going to hit the ball standing like that."

T he little frog didn't understand.

"What do you mean? How am I supposed to stand?" he asked. "And who are you anyway?"

"My name is Freddie," said the fly, as he buzzed in circles around the little frog. "You should bend forward with your head down, and never take your eyes off the ball until you hit it. And you need a caddie who can tell you which club to use, 'cause you're using the wrong one right now! Here, let me hold that bag for you."

The fly pulled out a different club and handed it to the little frog. "Okay, use this one and be careful not to hit it too far," he advised.

The little frog figured he had nothing to lose by trying, so he bent over the ball just like Freddie told him to. He hit the ball to the middle of the first lily pad on his first try. He said to Freddie, "That worked great! You sure are smart and you sure are fast. I'm going to call you 'Fast Freddie'!"

The little frog swam out to the pad and putted the ball right in the shell.

One of his sisters yelled from the bank, "Hey, Little Frog, how come you're not eating that fly?"

The little frog yelled back, "Because he's my new caddie!"

Sinking the putt hole after hole after hole, the little frog announced that he would never miss a putt again! Now there were hundreds of frogs gathered around the pond and they all roared in approval.

"He sure can putt that ball!"
yelled one of the frogs.

"He is the best putting frog I have ever seen!"
roared another.

The little frog's oldest brother replied proudly,

"That's right, because he's The Putter Frog!"

And from that day forward, the little frog was known as The Putter Frog. He continued to play golf every day, and just as he promised, he never missed a putt. The golf course he built became famous among all the frogs, tadpoles, and other creatures in the pond.

A few years later, Putter Frog stood at a podium in the middle of the eighteenth lily pad and declared, "I am dedicating the Frogmore International Golf Club to my parents, Mama and Papa Frog, because they believed in me and let me be the best putter in the world. Thanks, Mama and Papa! And, of course, a special thanks to my caddie, Fast Freddie!"

And that's the Legend of the Putter Frog!

Author's Note

Frogmore, SC, is named after Queen Victoria's home in England, Frogmore Manor. Nearby Penn Community Center was established after the Civil War to educate freed slaves and is where Dr. Martin Luther King, Jr. wrote his famous, "I Have A Dream," speech in the early 1960's. Beaufort, SC, Parris Island Marine Corps Recruit Depot, and Fripp Island are just a few miles away. A local airport, affectionately known as the Frogmore International Airport, was the inspiration for the Frogmore International Golf Club. Fred Bazemore, my best friend, owns Freddie's Pawn Shop in Beaufort and is nicknamed "Fast Freddie" because of his "fast" wheeling and dealing! Dataw Island, just two miles from Frogmore, is the home of one of the most beautiful golf courses in the United States and is where the Putter Frog was born.